Helen Moriarty

Idle rhymes

Helen Moriarty

Idle rhymes

ISBN/EAN: 9783337271053

Printed in Europe, USA, Canada, Australia, Japan

Cover: Foto ©Andreas Hilbeck / pixelio.de

More available books at **www.hansebooks.com**

IDLE RHYMES

BY

HELEN LOUISE MORIARTY

WITH

ILLUSTRATIONS BY F. C. LIND

CINCINNATI
The Robert Clarke Company Press
1895

Never did Poesy appear
  So full of Heaven to me, as when
I saw how it would pierce through pride and fear,
  To the lives of coarsest men.

It may be glorious to write
  Thoughts that shall glad the two or three
High souls, like those far stars that come in sight
  Once in a century;—

But better far it is to speak
  One simple word, which now and then
Shall waken their free nature in the weak
  And friendless sons of men!

                    —*James Russell Lowell.*

CONTENTS.

APOLOGIA.

A humble singer on a shadowy slope,
Begun one morn to chant a simple lay,
Weak was her voice, her harp not strung to
    play
Anthems sublime—she only sung of hope.

Too weak her voice to reach the bolder
    heights
Where laurel bends in green profusion round.
Where happy voices bid the air resound,
    And glorious singers taste of Fame's de-
    lights.

Too weak her voice and homely far her lays,
Toward themes intense her thoughts were never
    turned,
And yet within her soul such fires burned,
  As led the bards of old thro' triumph's ways.

And so she sung, nor had she wish to cope
With singers grand, whose anthems reach the
    skies.
Her only meed the praise in friendly eyes,
  This humble singer on a shadowy slope.

EASTER.

Hark ! To the tuneful glory
    Of Easter bells !
List ! To the old, old story
    Their music tells.
Clear on the air outpealing
    In joy sublime
Gently the words come stealing
    "' T is Easter time !"

Hark ! To the bells now singing
    The tale of Eld !
New hope to sad hearts bringing
    In bondage held.

List! For they sing, " O mortals,
  Be blind no more;
Enter the longed-for portals—
  God's open door!"

UNSATISFIED.

We sigh for Happiness, and when she's come
  With lagging step to meet us on our way,
Draped in strange garments, and with lips all
    dumb,
    And eyes that mock our actions, grave or
    gay :
We sigh again for visions that have vanished,
  The glorious image we had builded up,
Whose tender hands would skillfully have ban-
    ished
    The bitter dregs that lurk within our cup.

We sigh, perhaps, for Love, and when he halts
  Our hurrying footsteps with his magic darts,
We shrink and shudder at the rash assaults.
    Striving to hide our wounded, quivering
    hearts,
And sigh again, while from the echoing deeps,
  Rise the illusions of our life's young day :
Stifling within our souls the song that leaps

Like mountain stream to meet Love on his
    way.

.   .   .   .

We sigh again for Peace, O restless, weary
    sigh!
We sigh for Peace, and lo! she passes heed-
    less by!

PEACE.

Peace be to ye! Spake the Master, words that
ring the ages through.
Falling still on weary spirits, as the drops of
Heaven's own dew.

Peace be to ye! Still we hear it, tho' the cent-
uries gaunt have furled
Time's old flag above the ramparts of a doubt-
ing, struggling world.

Peace be to ye! Falls the message, and our
anxious hearts find rest,
Calmed are all the waves of sorrow surging
thro' the aching breast.

Peace be to ye! And forever! Peace may
    wander far away,
Comes she back to find us waiting, patiently
    the livelong day.

Comes she back to find us weeping, o'er a
    bruised and broken heart.
Till she folds her wings about us, sternly bid-
    ding grief depart.

Bright-winged Peace! The artist paints thee,
    as a maid of winsome face,
Sunlit hair, soft eyes that rival wintry stars in
    realms of space.

But no artist's gifted pencil can thy soothing
    power portray,
As thy words fall on our spirits like the fount-
    ain's welcome spray.

Peace, beloved of God, His angels guide thee
    with mysterious wands,
Into homes, where hearts are heavy, from the
    weight of sorrow's bands.

Guide thee where sad tears are falling, and the
    moan of breaking hearts,
Still is heard above the tumult in the World's
    deceptive marts.

'Tis thy work, for He has willed thee, 'mid
    Earth's desolate spots to roam,
Lifting Heavenward drooping spirits, lighting
    many a darkened home.

As thou floatest gently toward us, drying up
    our waste of tears,
In thy wake there looms a vision, Hope, thy
    sister sweet, appears.

ESTRANGED.

I had a friend I loved—
  Friend by the tie of blood.
By whom thro' time and change
  My heart's best wishes stood.
Though changes came
  And loosed the chain
That bound our love together,
  Mine walks alone,
  All unbeknown,
Through darkest wintry weather.

And she has found a love
  Stronger by far than mine,
To which her heart may cling
  Thro' storm and in sunshine.
But still I pray
  That, day by day,
As the years pass briefly on,
  Her life may be
  From sorrow free
Till the Heavenly day shall dawn.

O WISTFUL EYES!

O wistful eyes, where shadow lies
    That love can ne'er dispel!
O dainty lips, where Cupid sips,
    The nectar he loves well!
O radiant smile, a loving wile,
    That lures my heart away!
O warm, soft hand, whose least command,
    My will must e'er obey!

O eyes once bright, whose earthly light
    Fate quenched with ruthless hands,

Thy beauty hid, each fringèd lid
    Opes now in heavenly lands!
O tender heart, from thee to part
    Seems death!   My one relief
Thy glances sweet, in dreams to meet,
    Tho' waked again to grief.

O fair lost love, to thee above
    My fainting spirit calls!
Thy mem'ry here is like the tear,
    That trembling, never falls!
O eyes so blue, O heart so true,
    My best days died with thee,
And so I live on thoughts that give
    Thy image back to me.

TO A FRIENDLY SCRIBE.

Speak to your Muse about me,
　My Sprite has strayed away.
In new strange lands without me
　She takes her aërial way.
Often we strayed together,
　My fair lost Muse and I,
But in the wintry weather
　She sought a softer sky.

I fear me much I teased her,
　By careless ways and dreams.
My serious moods appeased her,
　And won her brightest gleams.
But still I held her lightly,
　And let my fancy stray
To hopes that shone so brightly—
　Alas, now flown away!

I fear, tho' she may wander
　In far and mystic ways,
She oft must rest and ponder
　On the sweet bygone days.

When dreaming, we searched the meadows
　　For the flowers of Poesie,
That grow in the deepest shadows,
　　By Life's immortal tree.

Speak to your Muse, when wooing
　　The strain you long to grasp.
Tell her of my undoing—
　　The Sprite I fain would clasp
Has fled to fields elysian.
　　When bathed in morning dew,
She stands. a beauteous vision,
　　To glad the chosen few.

Speak to your Muse when lingering
　　With Pan beside the sea,
You watch the magic fingering
　　That sets your fancy free.
Speak, while the listening ocean
　　Absorbs the wild refrain,
And tells in eternal motion
　　Its sweetness o'er again.

Speak, and your Muse attending
　　Shall wing her airy flight,
And far-off heights ascending
　　Shall find my wandering Sprite,

Who, listing then to the story—
    A soul's repentant say—
Will turn from the fields of glory
    To brighten my path alway.

TOO LATE.

Adown the lane he wandered in the gloaming ;
　　His step was slow, wistful and sad his eye.
To childhood's home, after long years of roam-
　　　　ing,
　　He was returning now, perhaps to die.

When first he left it life was fair, and joyous
　　Pleasures too many for his hands to grasp;

But joys once ours, too soon begin to cloy us,
  While some fore'er elude our eager clasp.

Fame came to him, in foreign lands he wooed
    her :
  But at her best she proved a fickle jade :
In vain for constant love he often sued her,
  Too many at her shrine their court had paid.

At length grown weary of the restless dreaming
  And fitful fortunes of the farce called life,
He turned his face toward that fair haven
    teeming
  With thoughts of youthful days debarred
    from strife.

The dear old home ! Once bright with happy
    laughter
  Of children clustered 'round the mother's
    knee,
Where romping games had made the brown
    old rafters
  Ring back gay echoes to their careless glee.

Will it be changed ? He ponders, pausing
    sadly,
  Dreading the turn that brings it to his view,
Calling to mind the day when turning gladly
  He waved his hand in one long, last adieu.

He rounds the turn—one look and all is ended.
  The hopes, the fears, that ever held a part
Of half-formed wishes that for years had blended
  With every quick pulsation of his heart!

This was the ending then of dreams and long-
    ings!
  These charred remains—that blackened heap
    of stone—
The moldering witnesses of last belongings,
  Mute. touching signs of what was once his
    home.

SONNET.

"Great souls attract sorrows, as mountains, tempests."—*Jean Paul Richter.*

Great souls are those whom Sorrow broods
  among.
High-souled herself, she tests them by her own,
That by repeated tests has greater grown,
Since first the narrow path her young feet trod,
Her trembling hands held by a loving God,
And won the crown, high from His throne out-
  flung.
The crown of Sorrow! Fashioned 'mid angels'
  tears,
Of shining leaves that hide the pricking thorn.
Fashioned for myriad children, yet unborn,
Whose heritage 't will be, that they may know
The price that Calvary paid to stem the flow
Of man's iniquities through all the years.
And knowing, learn the truth that sorrow
  brings,
The crown that glorifies, e'en hath its stings.

CONVENT ECHOES.

Clear on the air, their pulsing cadence pealing,
  I hear a sweet refrain,
While o'er my thoughts a mist is gently stealing,
  And mem'ries come again,

Of quiet halls where dusk is slow descending,
  Where peace has spread her wings.
Soft music in the distance only lending
  More charms where twilight clings.

Anon appear the black robed nuns, their faces
  Serene in sweet repose;
Across their brows the world has left no traces
  Of earthly dreams or woes.

Now loud on air the organ music swelling.
    They reach the chapel door—
The sweet faint incense stealing upward, telling
    'Tis Benediction's hour.

Now low-bowed heads, and hearts to Him
        ascending
    On incense laden air.
Ah surely Heaven must smile with ear attending
    The nuns' low whispered prayer.

Fond mem'ry lingers on those dim old hall-
        ways—
    Lingers and drops a tear,
And kind affection drapes the picture always
    Thro' each succeeding year.

MUSING.

Some fateful years drift silently and slow,
    Some quickly—for in youth the hours fly,
Bringing betimes to pleasure's cheek a glow,
    Betimes from wounded hearts the hopeless
        sigh.

To-day we laugh, and sun ourselves in Joy,
    But e'er to-morrow dawns that sun has set.
To-day contentment beams without alloy,
    To-morrow finds us in cold Sorrow's debt.

Cold Sorrow? Nay, we must not call her cold;
    Sweetness she brings to many a barren life,
Softness to many a hardened heart, and bold—
    Nay, reckless made because of ceaseless
        strife.

The sweetest singers by the world adored,
    Whose tuneful lyres in hist'ry play a part,
Were led by Sorrow's hand to where are stored
    The chords that touch the universal heart.

The tenderest hearts are those to sorrow wed,
　The sweetest roses in their bloom are crushed,
The noblest spirits in their prime lie dead.
　　The bitterest cries within our hearts are
　　　hushed.

Sweet Sorrow! At thy shrine awhile we pause
　To muse and murmur 'gainst this life of ours,
Paying sad tribute unto thy great cause,
　Then on again to worship happier powers.

Bending our knees at every wayside shrine.
　Chasing a phantom that we can not see,
Sighing for visions fair that ever shine,
　But come not near till opes eternity.

THE CORNER PORCH.

Upon the dear old corner porch,
   Under its sheltering care,
How oft in happy, joyous groups,
   We've breathed the summer air.
With mirthful jest and merry song
   The hours flew charmed away,
And days were bright and hearts were light
   And Pleasure held full sway.

Upon the dear old corner porch,
   When moonlight's shimmering haze

Was sifted downward thro' the trees.
  That watched our childish plays,
We've sat and sung in careless glee.
  And dreamed our youthful dreams.
And longed to launch our trembling craft
  On Life's alluring streams.

Those merry groups are scattered all,
  For, in the swath of years,
Who drank awhile from pleasure's cup
  Soon found it gemm'd with tears.
Some sailed afar, and in strange lands
  Their wandering steps are led,
And on the dear old corner porch
  Some laughed who now are dead.

Some sang upon the corner porch,
  All heedless of the day
When joy would turn to bitterness
  As flowers to decay.
Some staked affection's garnered wealth
  In love's bright golden wheel,
And lost, for life is full of strife,
  And dreams are never real.

Some played upon the corner porch—
  Ah me, those hallowed hours,
Secure and sweet are treasured up
  'Mong memory's fondest flowers.—

Who 've since attuned a stranger harp
    To sorrow's mournful lays,
Whose trembling chords are answering words,
    That meet across life's ways.

Upon the dear old corner porch
    As children we have played ;
Upon the dear old corner porch
    Some tender vows were made.
Around the dear old corner porch
    Our memories have cast
A halo bright, that gilds for us
    The days forever past.

"MANY ARE CALLED."

My Lord hath called me to His vineyard—hear
His low voice echo thro' the air so clear!
My Lord hath called me, but the day is young,
I fain would linger these sweet flowers among.

My Lord hath called me—but the morn is fair,
Its beauty lures me—shall I then compare
The fleeting joys that hold my soul in thrall
With work that waits me at His earnest call?

My Lord hath called me—I am coming soon.
I only wait until the heat of noon
Is past.   Then I shall meet His smile :
He will not miss me—I shall rest awhile.

My Lord hath called me—lo! the sun has gone!
The shadows lie where erst his rays had shone.
Fain would I labor while the light doth last :
Fain would I labor—but the day is past!

My Lord hath called me—and the eve is new,
The long day faded with the falling dew.
Still must I travel onward thro' the night.
Lord, Thou hast called me.   Help me in Thy
     might!

A JUNE MORNING.

On the soft grass Night's tears are resting
    lightly,
  And stealing onward comes the gentle
    Dawn :
With lingering footsteps like a timid maiden,
  Who in strange pathways wanders, wist-
    ful, on.

The air is heavy with a vap'rous sadness,
  The subtle sorrow of the dying Night :
Whose last faint breath on zephyr's wings borne
    forward
  Removes the veil that hides the sun's fair
    light.

Against the lightening sky the moon gleams
    palely,
  Her cold, bright charms eclipsed by morn-
    ing's King,
Who, thro' the mists his way triumphant pierc-
    ing,
  Soon o'er the waiting earth his radiance
    flings.

O fair June morning! Type of life's sweet
    moments!
  Brief as their fleeting beauty and as bright.
Untouched by latent fear of storm or sorrow,
  Too soon thou 'rt ended, leaving starless
    night!

SOME DAY.

Some day—some day, before this life is ended,
  Some bitter gloomful day,
When pain and sorrow through the long years
    blended,
  Have swept my strength away;
When life's illusions in the distance fading,
  So specter-like and dim,
Seem shadow-masts of that great ship whose
    lading
  Shall be my duty grim ;
I know that I shall welcome Death and greet
    him—
  Not with youth's fearful face,
But as a gentle friend, and haste to meet him,
  Freed from the world's embrace.

Some day. it may be while alone and friend-
    less,
  No loving face I see,
And the dark road that stretches off so endless
  Grows no small flower for me.
When fainting by the way, my spirit lingers
  On thoughts of other days,

Whose specters, pointing with their fleshless
    fingers,
  But urge me on my way :
When gloomy, dark, the future towers o'er me,
  Life's pyramid so vast—
Ah then shall Death, the Master, stand before
    me,
  And claim his own at last !

DOROTHY

Blythe and gay and sweet and winsome,
   Careless, happy, bright and free,
Always smiling, time beguiling,
   This is blue-eyed Dorothy.

Upstairs, downstairs, always running,
   Now to work and now to play,
Always teasing, always pleasing,
   This is Dot the livelong day.

Out to romp with chosen playmates,
  In to see how Mamma fares,
Always singing, comfort bringing,
  Lightening all the daily cares.

Then when twilight comes, slow, stealing,
  With its soft and silent tread,
Blue eyes closing, Dot is dozing,
  Drops to rest her curly head.

THE POET'S SONG.

I.

The Poet sung of love—his pulses stirred,
His heart kept time to every tender word ;
While Fancy conjured up a picture rare,
The one, to him, of all the world most fair,
Whose radiant smile for him alone beams sweet,
Whose loving glances make his fond heart beat.

II.

The Poet sung of love—his glorious theme
In answering hearts awoke a slumb'ring dream,
And mem'ries sprung to life, whose radiance
    blest
The somber present like a welcome guest ;
And lingering still, as twilight deepens fast,
Evoke the beauteous shades that graced the
    past.

III.

The Poet sung—but as his willing pen
The sweet words traced that spake his love
    again,

The light that shone in lifted eyes waxed dim.
And all the world grew dark the while for him.
Soon pæan song was turned to sorrow's dirge,
As grief's dark anchor did his soul submerge.

IV.

The Poet sung of Heav'n—and lo! there fell
Upon his spirit such a chastening spell,
Such deep, full peace—such joy as angels feel,
When forth their voices ring in glad appeal.
And still his songs re-echo through the years,
While hearts in sorrow read them o'er with
        tears.

A SNOWY NIGHT.

The snow still falls—the night is dark,
  The time drags weary footsteps on.
Falls the white pall o'er all the earth—
  The earth that waits the coming dawn.
Waited by some in joy and mirth,
  In happy homes—in stately halls.
Waited by others but to bring
  More grief within their lowly walls.

But 't is a soft and gentle cloak.
  This white, mysterious snow of ours:
Closely it clasps the grimy earth
  In frozen folds of wintry showers.

Closely enfolding like a Fate,
    Whose solemn ways we can not gauge ;
But like a Fate whose advent brings
    A balm that can our griefs assuage.

INCONSISTENCY.

O weary days of Sorrow—weary days,
  When e'en the sun shines with a luster lack,
You linger long, and still seem loth to go:
  And when you go, we fain would call you
    back,
To make our burdens greater with your woe,
  And plant your weeds 'mid pleasures shining
    bays.

CONTENTMENT.

Contentment! Precious gift that few possess!
When we possess you, then we love you less:
But when your balm our spirits sorely lack,
Ah then we sigh for you and wish you back!
Some few do know you and a few possess,
And some mistake you for kind happiness.
O blest mistake to him who labors in it!
To feign content doth oft times help to win it!

THOUGHTS AFTER A SERMON.

"Why stand'st thou idle here the long, long
    day ;
  Why stand'st thou here where pillars thee
    concealed ?"
Those words 'woke echoes in my heart to play
  Upon the chords which conscience left re-
    vealed.

Why stand'st thou idle here, why waste the
    time
  Which for His purposes the Lord hath lent
    thee ?

(46)

The hill of life is yet for thee to climb:
  Begin thy work, else all too late, repent
    thee!

Thy burdens may be many—yes, 't is true,
  But why shouldst thou exempt from bur-
    dens be?
Wouldst careless walk whilst all thy brethren
    sue
  For help, their way thro' dark'ning clouds
    to see?

Why like the Pharisee stand'st thou afar,
  Thanking thy God (stifling thy rising qualms)
That thou needst not thy peaceful lot to mar,
  By wailing prayers and penitential psalms?

Canst thou remember not those warning words,
  Which with great love thy Lord hath sent to
    thee?
Hast never to its depths thy soul been stirred?
  " Who humbleth himself shall yet exalted be!"

Ah soul, so erring in poor human lights,
  Which still the image of thy Maker beareth:
Retrace thy straying steps—a pathway bright.
  Choose, and Him seek who for thy welfare
    careth.

Doubt not, that He who notes a sparrow's fall
   Canst see thy fainting spirit helpless stand.
Doubt not, that at thy earliest, earnest call,
   He will outreach to thee a helping hand.

DREAMS.

We dream fair dreams by night—
  Day comes and swift they vanish.
They go, but leave behind a light,
  That sunshine can not banish.

Their shadows linger in the air—
  Their impress—what you will.
And tho' the dreams have flown fore'er,
  Their beauty mocks us still.

UNREST.

Play me a tender tune to night,
  My spirit longs for rest.
Repose hath fled mine eyelids quite,
  Play softly—that is best.

Play me a tender tune to-night,
  Its cadence sweet and slow,

Will fall upon my weary heart
  Like love-words whispered low.

Play me a tune in minor chords,
  And let the sweet refrain
Steal thro' my listening senses,
  Like happiness thro' pain.

For in thro' the murmuring music
  The plaintive air will creep,
Like the chorus that surges ever
  From the heart of the briny deep.

And as the monotoned murmur,
  From the depths of the sea that springs,
Has balm in its deeper music
  To loosen the bound heart-strings,

So the soft-toned minors blended
  With the sad and mournful air,
Will bring to the soul a message
  Of peace that is like a prayer.

So play me a tender tune to-night,
  Play softly, sweet and slow.
And phantom thoughts will glide away
  With the music's ebb and flow.

THE SLEEPER.

Across the cool, dim chamber, the deep'ning
    twilight stole,
The sun had long since sunk to rest within a
    crimson bowl.
Swathed in the rising moonlight the quiet
    sleeper lay
Asleep at last—a dreamless sleep—to last with
    her for aye!

Asleep at last! No phantom dreams disturb
    thy slumbers now!
Sin and the world have writ their last upon
    that marble brow!
The saddened impress of the years that found
    and left thee young,
A blighted life—a broken heart—a requiem
    unsung!

Hovering above that lonely couch with droop-
    ing wings outspread,
An angel of thy childish days keeps watch
    above thy head;
And chanting low the record of those gentlier,
    happier years,
He drops upon thy flitting soul his cleansing,
    pitying tears.

O wasted life! Fit type art thou of dreams
    that fade away,
And life's alluring blandishments, that live but
    for a day;
And hopes that bloom and promise fair, yet
    like thee die too soon,
As dies the pale young primrose with the wan-
    ing of the moon.

O fair pale form! O dead cold face! Calm
    now in Death's embrace,
Too soon thy feet grew weary in life's mad
    and bitter race ;
Too soon thy gentle spirit broke—too soon thy
    strength gave way !
Alas, that such things e'er must be as long as
    life holds sway !

So let us weep about thy couch before thou'rt
    laid away,
And violets plant above the mound that hides
    thy lonely clay;
Praying that winds like zephyrs light may ever
    gently sweep
Around that small and lowly home where thou
    dost peaceful sleep.

www.ingramcontent.com/pod-product-compliance
Lightning Source LLC
Chambersburg PA
CBHW021232260626
47172CB00002B/721